Hatching the Plan.

~~~

I started to think of a Plan.

I looked up at the clock. It would be hours before Aldo came in to clean Room 26.

So I took a big chance.

I jiggled the lock-that-doesn't-lock on my cage.

My friends all think the door is locked. They don't know that I can open it and get out.

"Don't worry, Og," I said. "I'll be right back."

Og splashed in his tank as I slid down the leg of the table and scampered across the floor. That part was easy.

Humphrey's
School Fair Surprise

Betty G. Birney
illustrated by **Priscilla Burris**

PUFFIN BOOKS

PUFFIN BOOKS
An Imprint of Penguin Random House LLC
375 Hudson Street, New York, NY 10014

First published in the United States of America by G. P. Putnam's Sons
and Puffin Books, imprints of Penguin Young Readers Group, 2016

THE LIBRARY OF CONGRESS HAS CATALOGED
THE G. P. PUTNAM'S SONS EDITION AS FOLLOWS:
Birney, Betty G.
Humphrey's school fair surprise / Betty G. Birney ;
illustrated by Priscilla Burris.
pages cm.—(Humphrey's tiny tales ; 4)
Summary: "The students of Room 26 are so excited for Longfellow School's
big school fair! Pet hamster Humphrey is too—but will he be allowed to
march in the parade with his classmates?"—Provided by publisher.
[1. Hamsters—Fiction. 2. Pets—Fiction. 3. Fairs—Fiction. 4. Schools—Fiction.]
I. Burris, Priscilla, illustrator. II. Title.
PZ7.B5229Hv 2016
[Fic]—dc23 2014044988
ISBN 978-0-399-17229-8 (hardcover)
Printed in the United States of America
Puffin Books ISBN 978-0-14-751460-8
5 7 9 10 8 6 4

Design by Ryan Thomann.
Text set in ITC Stone Informal Std Medium.

Contents

Surprising News

I've learned a lot about school in the short time I've lived in one.

As a classroom hamster, I get to see and hear everything that goes on in Room 26.

One thing I've learned is that it's important to listen to our teacher, Mrs. Brisbane. She is super smart. She's a good teacher, too.

I've also learned that it's important to listen to Mr. Morales, the principal. Mr. Morales is the Most Important Person at Longfellow School.

One Monday, when he came into our classroom, he said something VERY-VERY-VERY important. It was also quite surprising.

"As you know, class, the Longfellow School Fair is coming up on Saturday," he said.

My friends got very excited.

"Will there be cotton candy?" Heidi Hopper asked.

She forgot to raise her hand.

I think of her as Raise-Your-Hand-Heidi because Mrs. Brisbane always has to remind her to do it.

Mr. Morales smiled. "I think so," he said.

A.J. remembered to raise his

hand, and Mr. Morales called on him.

"WILL THERE BE CUPCAKES?" A.J. asked.

A.J.'s voice is very loud, so I call him Lower-Your-Voice-A.J.

Mr. Morales said there would be cupcakes. There would also

be games and crafts and things that sounded like hamster-iffic fun.

"Yippee!" I shouted.

Of course, all that my friends heard was a very loud "Squeak!"

"This year, we are adding something new," Mr. Morales told us. "And everyone will be part of it."

"Are you listening, Og?" I squeaked to my neighbor.

Og is a frog. He lives in a tank right next to my cage on a long table by the window.

Since I can't see his ears, I'm never sure if he's listening or not.

"BOING-BOING!" he answered in his funny voice.

I guess he really was listening.

"During the fair, each class will march around the playing field," Mr. Morales said.

"Oooh," my classmates said.

"You'll all make signs that will show what makes Room Twenty-six special," Mr. Morales explained. "There will be a prize given for the best class spirit."

"Oooh," my classmates said again.

"Do you think Room Twenty-six will win the prize?" Mrs. Brisbane asked the class.

Every student shouted "Yes!" including me.

Og splashed around in the water side of his tank.

After Mr. Morales left, I was so happy, I hopped on my wheel for a fast spin.

I should have listened to the teacher, but I couldn't stop thinking about the school fair.

~~~~~~

Og and I were alone during recess. "The fair sounds great, doesn't it?" I asked.

"BOING-BOING!" Og answered.

"Cupcakes sound yummy. And games are fun!" I squeaked.

"BOING-BOING-BOING!" Og said.

"I just have one question, Og. What *is* a school fair?" I asked.

Og dived into the water and swam away from my cage. I guess he didn't know what a school fair was, either.

But I wasn't worried. I knew I'd find out VERY-VERY-VERY soon.

~~~~~

My friends were all talking when they came back to the classroom.

I heard them say some very odd things.

"Beanbags," Garth said.

Gail giggled and shouted, "Sponges!"

Gail loves to giggle, but I had never heard her laugh about sponges before.

Sayeh, who hardly ever speaks, smiled and said, "Face painting!"

"Class, we have work to do," Mrs. Brisbane said. "We need to think about our signs. What do you think makes our class special?"

Lots of hands went up.

"We learn a lot of important things in Room Twenty-six," Mandy said.

I agreed with that. I'd even learned to read and write in Room 26, which is unusual for a hamster.

"We've got the best teacher," Richie said.

That made Mrs. Brisbane smile. "But other classes have nice teachers and learn a lot," she said. "Is there anything that sets this class apart from the others?"

Miranda Golden raised her hand. I think of her as Golden-Miranda because of her golden hair.

"We have the nicest students," she said with a smile.

She was RIGHT-RIGHT-RIGHT! I was lucky to be in a class with such nice humans.

"Here is a different way to look at it," Mrs. Brisbane said. "What do we have that no other class has?"

I looked around the room.

There was a colorful bulletin board with pictures of important people on it. I didn't know who they were, but I was sure they were important.

I looked
some more
and saw
books,

pencils, paper and maps.

My friends glanced around the
room, too.

Suddenly, Heidi
said, "Humphrey!"
(She forgot to
raise her hand
again.)

Then A.J. shouted, "And Og!"

The class was buzzing with excitement.

Mrs. Brisbane clapped her hands to quiet everyone down. "Quiet, please," she said. "I agree, no other class has a hamster like Humphrey and a frog like Og. Should we use them on our signs?"

I was too surprised to squeak up, but my classmates all cheered.

Even Og said, "BOING!"

"We will start working on them tomorrow," Mrs. Brisbane said.

BUSY-BUSY-BUSY

The next morning, after math and reading, Mrs. Brisbane gave each student a large piece of cardboard.

"It's time to make our signs," she said.

My friends all went to work drawing and writing on those blank pieces of cardboard.

From my cage by the window, it was hard to make out what their signs looked like.

Room 26
is
hamster-
iffic!

Room 26
is
frog-tastic!

GO,
OG!

They couldn't finish them in one day, so the next day, they worked on them again.

By lunchtime, I could finally see what they had done.

Richie's sign read: *Room 26 is hamster-iffic!*

Art's said: *Room 26 is frog-tastic!*

That means they think that Og and I are terrific and fantastic. That made me feel GOOD-GOOD-GOOD.

There were other great signs, too. Miranda's read: *Humphrey rules!*

Sayeh's sign said: *Go, Og!* That's funny, because Og is "go" spelled backward.

Tabitha and Kirk made signs that read *Hamster Power* and *Frogs Rule!*

The signs were every color of the rainbow. Some had flowers

and glitter. Some had funny pictures of Og and me.

All of them made me proud to be in Room 26!

~~~~~

At the end of the day, after science, my friends made ears.

YES-YES-YES! They took paper, scissors, crayons and glue and made little hats with hamster ears sticking up.

It was funny to see my human friends wearing hamster ears. (They didn't make frog ears

because, as I said, frogs don't have ears that you can see.)

"You've done a wonderful job," Mrs. Brisbane told the class. "Tomorrow we'll practice marching."

Late that afternoon, Og and I were alone in the classroom. I looked out at all the signs.

"Don't they look great?" I asked Og. "They must be the best in the school!"

"BOING!" Og said. I knew he agreed with me.

"I wish I had a sign," I said.

"BOING-BOING!" Og said.

I liked doing everything my friends in Room 26 did. But if I carried a sign, it would have to be a teeny-tiny one.

25

I started to think of a Plan.

I looked up at the clock. It would be hours before Aldo came in to clean Room 26.

So I took a big chance.

I jiggled the lock-that-doesn't-lock on my cage.

My friends all think the door is locked. They don't know that I can open it and get out.

"Don't worry, Og," I said. "I'll be right back."

Og splashed in his tank as I slid down the leg of the table and scampered across the floor. That was the easy part.

Finding the art supplies to make a sign wouldn't be so easy.

There's an open space under each tabletop where my friends keep their supplies. But it's really hard for a small hamster to reach that space.

Then I noticed that Richie had left his jacket hanging over the back of his chair.

Mrs. Brisbane wouldn't like that, but I did.

I was able to stand on my tippy toes and reach UP-UP-UP to grab the sleeve with my paws.

I held on tightly and slowly climbed up the sleeve. Then, *1-2-3*, I leaped onto the seat of Richie's chair.

I stood on the edge of the chair and reached UP-UP-UP. I grabbed the collar of the jacket and pulled myself into the open space.

Oh, what treasures I found there.

Crayons, markers, pencils.

A ruler, scissors, glue.

Books and paper.

How I wished I had a desk like that!

"BOING-BOING-BOING," Og called out as a warning.

I looked over at the window. It was getting dark.

I poked around quickly and found what I was looking for: a teeny-tiny square of brown cardboard.

Richie was a very nice boy.

I was pretty sure he wouldn't mind if I took it.

Then I remembered that Og might like a sign, too.

So I poked around some more until I found another teeny-tiny square of cardboard.

"BOING!" Og called out again. "BOING-BOING-BOING!"

He was right. There was no time to waste.

I put the cardboard squares in my mouth. Then I jumped down to the chair, grabbed onto the sleeve of Richie's coat and slid to the ground.

Oops! I landed on the floor with a big THUMP.

I raced toward the table.

I can't slide *up* the table leg, so I grabbed the cord hanging down from the blinds. I swung on it and swung

some more until I was level with the tabletop. Then I let go.

I zoomed across the table, right up to Og's tank.

"I'll make a great sign for you," I promised him.

Suddenly, I heard footsteps coming down the hall toward Room 26.

"BOING!" Og said.

I hurried to my cage and pulled the door behind me. The lock-that-doesn't-lock clicked into place just in time. No one would know I had ever gotten out of my cage.

I tucked the cardboard under some of my bedding.

The door to Room 26 opened and the lights went on.

"Aldo's here to bring you cheer!" a friendly voice said. Aldo wheeled his cleaning cart into the room.

"How are my favorite class-room pets?" he asked.

"Great!" I said.

"BOING!" Og answered.

Aldo glanced around the room. "Uh-oh. Richie forgot his jacket," he said. "I'll have to talk to him about that."

Aldo is Richie's uncle.

As he swept and dusted, he talked to us. "Guess what, fellows?" Aldo asked.

"What?" I squeaked back.

"I signed up to be in the wet sponge booth for the school fair," he said.

I was squeakless. What on earth was a wet sponge booth?

"Yep. People pay money to throw wet sponges at some of the folks who work at the school," he said. "I think even Mr. Morales signed up."

I couldn't imagine anyone throwing a sponge at the principal *or* the custodian.

"Anything to help make money for Longfellow School," he said.

I could see his point, but I hoped no one would throw a wet sponge at me. After all, hamsters should NEVER-NEVER-NEVER get wet!

Og probably wouldn't mind, since he spends half his time in the water side of his tank.

When Aldo finished cleaning, he left the blinds open so the light from the streetlamp came in the room.

It was time for me to get to work.

I pulled the cardboard squares out from under the bedding. I reached behind the little mirror in my cage, where I hide my small notebook and pencil.

This time, all I needed was the pencil.

And something to write.

It's Not Fair!

It took me almost all night to think of what to write on the signs. Luckily, hamsters like me are wide-awake at night.

At first I tried to come up with something clever, like *hamster-iffic* or *frog-tastic*. But I couldn't.

I thought of writing *Room 26 is the BEST-BEST-BEST class in the whole school and the whole world!* But it wouldn't fit on the tiny piece of cardboard.

As it started to get light outside, I decided to keep it simple.

I wrote, *I ♡ Room 26!*

And on Og's sign, I wrote, *I ♡ Room 26, too!*

I thought they were perfect.

On Thursday afternoon, Mrs. Brisbane said it was time to finish the signs for the parade. She had brought long sticks so the students could hold up their signs.

Oops! I didn't have any sticks for our signs.

"Sorry, Og!" I told my neighbor. "I'll get some tonight."

Once the sticks were attached to the signs, my friends marched around the classroom, carrying them.

"They look
wonderful,"

Mrs. Brisbane said.

"Hold them high."

Room 26
is
hamster-
iffic!

Humphrey
rules!

"Shouldn't we say something when we are marching in the parade?" Raise-Your-Hand-Heidi said.

"Like what?" Mrs. Brisbane asked.

Heidi wasn't sure, but Speak-Up-Sayeh had an idea.

Sayeh doesn't like to talk, and when she does, she speaks in a soft voice. And everyone—including me—thinks she is NICE-NICE-NICE.

"We could say something

about Room Twenty-six," she said.

Garth said, "Yeah. Something about Humphrey and Og."

That idea got my whiskers wiggling!

Soon, all my friends were making up sayings about Room 26.

"Humphrey-Humphrey,
Og-Og!
We've got a hamster
and a frog!"

And:

"*BOING-BOING,*

SQUEAK-SQUEAK,

Og and Humphrey—

hear them speak!"

But they finally decided on:

"*Humphrey and Og*

are so much fun,

they make our class

number one!"

They marched around the

classroom again. I was so excited, I squeaked along with them.

"Humphrey and Og
are so much fun,
they make our class
number one!"

It was thrilling!

Mrs. Brisbane finally had my friends sit back down. "Thank you for such good work," she said. "On Saturday, we'll all meet by the bouncy castle at two o'clock and line up for the parade."

Kirk raised his hand. "Who will bring Humphrey and Og?" he asked.

Mrs. Brisbane looked surprised. "Bring them where?"

"To the parade," Kirk said.

Mandy, Miranda and Richie all raised their hands and said they'd bring us.

Mrs. Brisbane shook her head. "I'm sorry. Humphrey and Og can't be in the parade. It would be too dangerous."

I could see how sorry my friends were. But no one was

more disappointed than I was.

Og dived down into the bottom of his water. I think he was upset, too.

Golden-Miranda asked why it would be dangerous.

Mrs. Brisbane explained that I was too small to march in a parade, and if someone carried me, I might get hurt.

She said that Og certainly couldn't march and he needed to be near water.

She also said that it was supposed to be a hot, sunny day. The hot sun is not good for hamsters.

Everything she said made sense, but I still felt SAD-SAD-SAD.

So did my friends.

"Maybe they could ride," Garth suggested. "We could pull them in a wagon."

Now *that* was a good idea.

"There's still the sun," Mrs.

Brisbane said. "I'm worried about Humphrey."

"He could wear a hat," Stop-Giggling-Gail said. Then she giggled.

Everyone else giggled, too.

I guess a hamster would look pretty funny wearing a hat.

"I know!" Mandy said. "He could have an umbrella."

Everyone giggled at the thought of a hamster holding an umbrella, too.

"I'm sorry," Mrs. Brisbane said. "I don't think Humphrey and Og can be in the parade. But everyone will know about them because of the signs."

She moved on to talking about cleaning up the classroom.

I moved on to thinking about the school fair.

The school fair I would never see.

～～～

"It isn't fair, Og," I said after school had ended for the day. "It isn't fair that we can't go to the fair."

"BOING!" Og said. He didn't sound very cheery.

I hopped onto my wheel and took a good, long spin.

Spinning usually helps me feel better. It didn't help much that afternoon, though.

That night, when Aldo came in the room to clean, he said, "Sorry, guys! Richie called me up and said you can't go to the school fair."

"It's true!" I squeaked.

Aldo leaned on his broom and shook his head. "That doesn't seem right."

He started sweeping, but he kept on talking. "That's not fair. You two are a big part of this class. There must be a way. I'll think of something."

I was glad that Aldo wanted to help, but Mrs. Brisbane is our teacher. And if she says no to something, she means no.

Before he left, Aldo gave me a treat: a tiny little carrot stick.

Normally, I'd be happy to eat such a yummy treat. But this time, I had a better idea.

I pulled my tiny sign out from under my bedding. I carefully nibbled the top of the carrot to make a space just wide enough for the cardboard. The sign fit right in.

I lifted it up and it worked!

I marched across my cage and squeaked the class chant:

"Humphrey and Og
are so much fun,
they make our class
number one!"

That didn't sound right coming from me.

Then I thought of another one:

"Hey, hey—
the great school fair,
I'm so sorry
I won't be there!"

"BOING-BOING!" Og said. He leaped into the water with a huge splash.

I knew that he was sorry he wouldn't be there, either.

I always looked forward to going home with a different student each weekend. But on Friday, Mrs. Brisbane told me I would spend the night in the classroom.

"After all, everyone in class will be coming to the school fair tomorrow," she said. "You'd be left alone in someone's house. So after the fair, I'll take you home."

"Fine with me!" I squeaked.

Mrs. Brisbane laughed.

~~~~~

Aldo came in to clean that night. I didn't even know he cleaned on Friday nights!

"Humphrey, am I glad to see you," he said. "Because tonight, I have lots to do."

Aldo always had a lot to do. But that night, he worked so fast, it made my head spin.

When the room was clean, he

said, "I'm not
finished yet."

First, Aldo measured
my cage.

Next, he measured Og's tank.

Then he measured the top of
his cleaning cart.

He wrote some things down. "Great," he said. "Everything will be finished in time for the fair tomorrow."

"WHAT-WHAT-WHAT are you squeaking about?" I asked.

Aldo didn't answer. He pushed his cleaning cart out the door.

"What was that all about, Og?" I asked.

Og didn't answer. I guess he didn't know, either.

After Aldo was gone, I pulled my little sign out from under the bedding. It was a very nice sign. I was sorry I wouldn't get to carry it at the school fair.

So I ate the carrot.

My Big Surprise

Saturday morning, I woke up in Room 26. But it wasn't like any school day I'd ever known.

First, when Mrs. Brisbane unlocked the door, her husband, Bert, was with her.

"I can't wait to show you the signs," she said.

While Mrs. Brisbane went to get the signs, Mr. Brisbane wheeled his wheelchair over to the window.

"Hi, Humphrey! Hi, Og,"

he said.

"Good morning," I squeaked.

When Mr. Brisbane saw the signs, he said my friends had done a great job.

"Yes," Mrs. Brisbane said. "But they'll be sad if they don't win."

Mr. Brisbane put on a hamster-head hat and looked very silly.

Next, A.J. and Garth rushed in. They were SO-SO-SO excited.

"Richie said to meet him here," A.J. said. "He said it was important."

"I haven't seen him yet," Mrs. Brisbane told him.

Sayeh and Miranda came into the room.

"Where's Richie?" Miranda said. "He said he had something to show us."

Soon, most of my classmates were in Room 26, all looking for Richie. But Richie still wasn't there.

"I hope he comes soon," Mandy said. "I don't want to miss the face painting."

Just as everyone was about to give up, the door opened and Richie entered. Aldo was right behind him, pushing his cleaning cart.

I didn't know that Aldo cleaned on Saturdays, too!

"Wait till you see what Uncle Aldo made," Richie said.

Everyone gathered around Aldo and the cart, even Mr. and Mrs. Brisbane.

Of course, I couldn't see very well from the table by the

window. So I climbed up to the tippy top of my cage to get a better look.

"I thought of a way Humphrey and Og could march with you," Aldo said.

I was so surprised, I almost forgot to hold on to the cage.

"Would you like to see how?" Aldo asked.

"Oh, yes," Mrs. Brisbane said, and everyone agreed.

Aldo came over to the window and lifted my cage. "I'll be

careful with you, Humphrey," he told me.

He gently placed my cage on a board he had put on the top of the cart. My cage slid into slots on the board that were just the right size.

"See? I fixed it so his cage won't slide around," Aldo said.

"Very clever," Mrs. Brisbane said.

She was right!

Next, Aldo got Og's tank and set it in another spot on the

board. "Og's tank will stay firmly in place, too," he said.

"BOING!" Og said. He sounded very happy.

"Yes, but what about the hot sun?" Mrs. Brisbane asked.

Aldo didn't say a word. He just took out a big umbrella and put the handle in another slot on the board.

"They'll be in shade the whole time," he said. "What do you think?"

Of course, my friends thought

it was a GREAT-GREAT-GREAT idea.

But Mrs. Brisbane was the teacher. It was up to her.

"I think it will be fine for Humphrey and Og to march with us," she said. "Thank you, Aldo."

"THANKS-THANKS-THANKS, Aldo!" I squeaked.

Everybody laughed.

~~~~

While Mrs. Brisbane and my friends raced out of the classroom to enjoy the fair, Mr. Brisbane and Aldo stayed behind.

"We need to make a sign for the cart," Mr. Brisbane said.

The two men worked together and soon made a large sign that

read: *Og the Frog and Humphrey the Hamster.*

I liked it a lot. So did Og.

"I think you two deserve treats," Aldo said.

He gave Og a cricket. Yuck!

Then he gave me a tiny carrot stick. Yum!

As Aldo reached in my cage, he suddenly stopped. "What's this?"

Then he pulled out one of the little signs hidden in my bedding.

"'I love Room Twenty-six,'" he read. "Hey, somebody made Humphrey a sign! Oh, and Og has one, too."

"You're right," I squeaked. "But I ate my stick."

"These would be great signs if they had sticks," Aldo said.

He always seemed to know what I was thinking.

Before I knew it, Aldo had inserted tiny toothpicks in the signs. He attached one to my cage and one to Og's tank.

"I think we're ready to go," Mr. Brisbane said.

He was right. I was READY-READY-READY.

The hallway whizzed by us as Aldo rolled the cart down the hall. Mr. Brisbane rolled along next to us.

"Hey, Og, we're going to the school fair!" I squeaked. I could hardly believe it.

Aldo rolled us out the door, out to the playground.

I'd only seen the playground once before.

I'd seen swings and a slide and lots of open space. But today, the playground looked completely different.

"What do you think, fellows?" Aldo asked as he pushed us through the crowd.

What did I think? I thought it was amazing!

The open space was filled with people and the most wonderful sights I'd ever seen.

I looked to my right and saw Garth throwing a beanbag at a board with rows of holes. He got one into a hole that said three points.

Everybody cheered.

"Yay, Garth!" I squeaked. I

doubt if anyone heard me over all the other noise.

I looked to my left and saw a booth filled with yummy treats of every size and shape.

We moved along and I saw a huge purple castle with children bouncing up and down inside.

"That looks like fun, doesn't it, Og?" I asked my neighbor.

Og just stared at the crowds with his big frog eyes.

Mrs. Brisbane came up with a small tiger. At least I thought it was a tiger.

But it turned out to be Sayeh, painted to look like a tiger.

"I got my face painted," she said with a happy smile.

I wasn't interested in getting my face painted. But it would be fun to be a tiger, at least for a day.

Aldo said he had to go to

the wet sponge booth, so Mrs. Brisbane said she'd push the cart.

"I don't want to miss this," she said.

She wheeled us past more booths and tables, with games and things to eat.

There was a big crowd gathered around the next booth.

Everyone was laughing at something, but I couldn't see what.

"I'll have a look, Og," I shouted to my friend.

I climbed up to the tippy top of my cage, where I hung from one paw.

I saw a big board with a hole in it. Sticking through the hole was Mr. Morales's head!

I was astonished to see my friend Golden-Miranda toss a wet sponge right at his face.

Splat! The sponge hit him on the cheek.

I was SHOCKED-SHOCKED-SHOCKED that anyone would treat the principal like that.

But the most amazing part

was that Mr. Morales was laughing!

"Who's next?" he shouted. "Help us raise money for new playground equipment."

So what looked like a very bad thing turned out to be a very good thing.

"Should I give it a try?" Mrs. Brisbane asked.

"Sure," Mr. Brisbane answered. "It's all for a good cause."

I never thought I'd see the day when my teacher would throw a wet sponge at the Most

Important Person at Longfellow School.

But she did.

As the crowd cheered, she pulled her arm back and let the sponge fly.

It hit him right on the nose.

Everybody laughed, even Mr. Morales.

School fairs were fun, all right.

They were also very surprising.

I Surprise Myself

When Mr. Morales left the booth to get ready for the parade, people started throwing wet sponges at Aldo.

The first one hit him right on the forehead. Aldo laughed so hard, water flew off his mustache.

Mrs. Brisbane went to get the signs for our class. She left Miranda in charge of Og and me.

"It's almost time for the parade, Humphrey," Miranda said. She wheeled us to the bouncy castle.

Soon Mrs. Brisbane was handing out signs to all my friends.

"Look at me, Humphrey," someone said.

I looked up and saw a giant
hamster!

"It's me—Art," the
giant hamster said. "I
had my face painted
like a hamster!"
I was HAPPY-HAPPY-HAPPY
to see that it really was Art.

"Hi, Humphrey," another
voice said.

A huge green face was
coming over.

"It's Mandy," the
green face said. "But
I bet I look like Og!"

"BOING-BOING!" Og said. He sounded happy.

Everyone lined up with their signs. My other classmates looked wonderful wearing their hamster-ear hats.

Mrs. Brisbane told the students to march in two straight lines, holding their signs high.

"When we get to the stage, A.J., you lead the chant," she said. "Everyone will be able to hear you."

She told Miranda and Kirk to push the cart together.

I heard a loud whistle that made my whiskers wiggle. Then I heard a band playing.

"All right, students. Forward march!" Mrs. Brisbane said.

The cart lurched forward.

"We're in a parade!" I told Og.

As we marched along, there were moms and dads, brothers and sisters, and even grandparents waving at us and cheering.

"There's Humphrey!" a small voice called out.

It was Garth's little brother, Andy.

Signs in the illustration: "GO Humphrey", "Hamster OG", "Room 26 is hamster-iffic!", "humphrey", "FROGS RULE!", "ROOM 26 RULES!", "Humphrey rules!"

Sometimes
we moved forward.
Sometimes we had to stop
while my friends marched in
place.

"Signs high! Here we go, A.J.!"
Mrs. Brisbane said.

We marched toward a wooden
stage on the edge of the playing
field.

"Let's surprise them, Humphrey," Kirk said.

I was surprised when he opened the door to my cage and reached inside to pick up my hamster ball.

I was even more surprised when he picked me up and put me inside the ball.

"Get out there where they can see you," he said.

"Go, Humphrey!" Miranda said.

Kirk set me on the ground in front of him.

I looked UP-UP-UP and saw Mr. Morales and some other important-looking people sitting on the stage, watching.

I heard A.J.'s loud voice lead the others.

"Humphrey and Og
are so much fun,
they make our class
number one!"

"Go, Humphrey, go!" I heard Garth yell.

I started walking, which made my ball spin off to the side.

At first it spun in a circle.

"Go, Humphrey, go!" The whole class was shouting now.

I started running. My ball started rolling forward, away from the class.

"Go, Humphrey, go!" the whole crowd yelled.

My ball rolled a little faster.

Large feet moved out of the way to let me pass.

I was moving FAST-FAST-FAST.

"Whoa, Humphrey! Come back!" I heard A.J. shout.

I heard footsteps running behind me.

My ball rolled past lots of feet and kept on going.

"Stop, Humphrey, stop!" I heard the crowd yell.

I stopped moving my feet. But a hamster ball doesn't have brakes, so it kept rolling.

I rolled and rolled and rolled some more. The trees and grass were just a blur.

I wondered how far a hamster ball could roll. Could it go on forever?

If I could have gone back, I would have.

All of a sudden, the ball stopped short. I flip-flopped a few times.

When I came to a stop, I looked up. A huge foot was right on top of my hamster ball!

Then a huge hand reached down and picked it up.

"Who have we got here?" the man holding the ball said.

By then, the crowd had caught up with me.

I heard Mrs. Brisbane's voice say, "Thank you for saving Humphrey, Officer Jones."

A large eye stared down at my hamster ball. "I should probably

give this hamster a ticket for speeding," Police Officer Jones said. "But I'll let him go with a warning this time."

Everybody laughed except me. I was way too tired to laugh.

Kirk came running up. He looked VERY-VERY-VERY worried.

"What were you thinking, Kirk?" Mrs. Brisbane asked.

"I'm sorry. I didn't think the ball would roll so far away," he said. Then he looked down at me. "I'm so sorry, Humphrey. I made a big mistake. I wouldn't want anything bad to happen to you."

I don't want anything bad to happen to me, either. But I know Kirk would never want to hurt me.

Mrs. Brisbane took me back to the stage.

Mr. Morales and all my friends were waiting there.

"This has been a very surprising fair," Mr. Morales announced.

That was TRUE-TRUE-TRUE.

"Thanks to our friend Humphrey, I don't think there will ever be another fair like it," he continued.

Everybody laughed except Og and me.

I was still too tired to laugh. Maybe Og was tired, too.

"So, for their great signs, their terrific hamster hats and their special classroom pets, I'm awarding the prize for best classroom spirit to Room Twenty-six!" he said.

My tiny ears twitched with all the clapping and cheering that followed.

Then Mr. Morales gave each student in Room 26 a free ticket for the bouncy castle. As you can imagine, my friends were excited about that.

"Thanks, Humphrey," Sayeh said.

"You're the best," A.J. told me.

"You're number one!" Miranda said.

Then my friends all left for castle bouncing and cotton candy, for face painting and cupcakes.

I didn't have a ticket, but that was fine with me. I'd had enough adventure for one day. I was ready for a nice long nap.

"Well, Og," I said, right before I dozed off, "school fairs are even more surprising than I thought. Don't you agree?"

My eyes were already closing when I heard a very loud "BOING-BOING-BOING!"

Look for the next
Humphrey chapter book

Humphrey's
Mixed-Up Magic Trick